P9-BZR-120

Juvenile

SCHAUMBURG TOWNSHIP DISTRICT LIBRARY

3 1257 01477 9796

WITHDRAWN

Schaumburg Township District Library

130 South Roselle Road

Schaumburg, Illinois 60193

JANE DYER

Little Brown Bear Won't Go to School!

SCHAUMBURG TOWNSHIP DISTRICT LIBRARY
JUVENILE DEPT.
130 SOUTH ROSELLE ROAD
SCHAUMBURG, ILLINOIS 60193

LITTLE, BROWN AND COMPANY

New York ✄ An AOL Time Warner Company

EASY
DYER, J

3 1257 01477 9796

Other Little Brown Bear Titles:
Little Brown Bear Won't Take a Nap!

Copyright © 2002 by Jane Dyer

All rights reserved. No part of this book may be reproduced in any form or by any electronic
or mechanical means, including information storage and retrieval systems, without permission in
writing from the publisher, except by a reviewer who may quote brief passages in a review.

First Edition

Library of Congress Cataloging-in-Publication Data
Dyer, Jane.
  Little Brown Bear won't go to school / Jane Dyer. — 1st ed.
    p. cm.
  Summary: Little Brown Bear does not want to go to school, so he tries various jobs
instead.
  ISBN 0-316-19685-1
  [1. Bears — Fiction. 2. Schools — Fiction. 3. Work — Fiction.] I. Title.
PZ7.D977 Lg 2003
[E] — dc21   2002034132

10 9 8 7 6 5 4 3 2 1

SCP

Manufactured in China

The illustrations for this book were done in Winsor and Newton watercolor
on Waterford 140-lb. hot press paper.

The text was set in Usherwood, and the display type is P22 Garamouche.

For Cecily

"I won't go to school," announced Little Brown Bear.
"Don't be silly," said Mama Bear. "Every little bear goes to school. Now finish your breakfast."
"You and Papa don't go to school," said Little Brown Bear.
"We're not little," said Mama Bear.
"Besides," said Papa Bear, "we have jobs."

"I want a job," said Little Brown Bear.

"Your job is to go to school," said Mama Bear as she handed him his schoolbag.

"Our job is to go to work," said Papa Bear. "So off we go!"

When they reached the school, Little Brown Bear waved good-bye to Papa Bear and blew Mama Bear a kiss. As he turned to go inside, he smelled pancakes smothered with butter and maple syrup. Instead of going inside, he tiptoed past his classroom and went next door to the Miss Flo Diner.

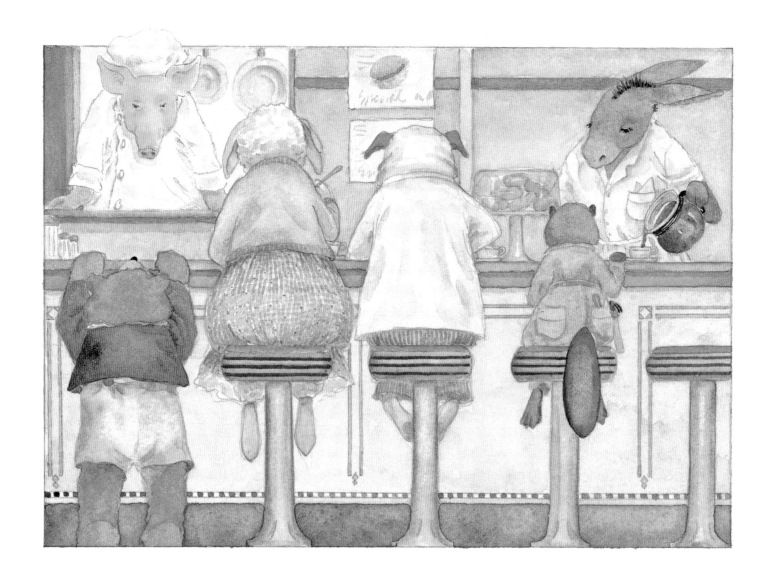

"Why aren't you in school?" asked the cook.

"I'm looking for a job," said Little Brown Bear.

"Hmmm," said the cook. "Can you take orders?"

"Oh, yes!" said Little Brown Bear.

The cook handed him a pad of paper. "Go to the first booth and find out what they want."

Little Brown Bear did just that and handed the order to the cook.

"I can't read this!" shouted the cook.
"Well, I don't know how to write,"
explained Little Brown Bear.

Little Brown Bear continued down the road until he spotted some beavers. They looked very busy.

"I'm looking for a job," Little Brown Bear said.
"We can always use another paw," said one beaver.

Little Brown Bear got right to work.
He sawed and he hammered.

But no matter how hard he tried, his wall always looked crooked.

Little Brown Bear decided to head back to town. Soon he came to a shop with the door ajar. He poked his head in and said, "I'm looking for a job."

A sheep looked up and asked, "What do you know about knitting?"

"Everything," said Little Brown Bear. He had watched Mama knit many times.

"Lovely," said the sheep. "I need help with these scarves."

Little Brown Bear picked up the wool and the needles and tried to knit. But instead he became more and more tangled in the yarn.

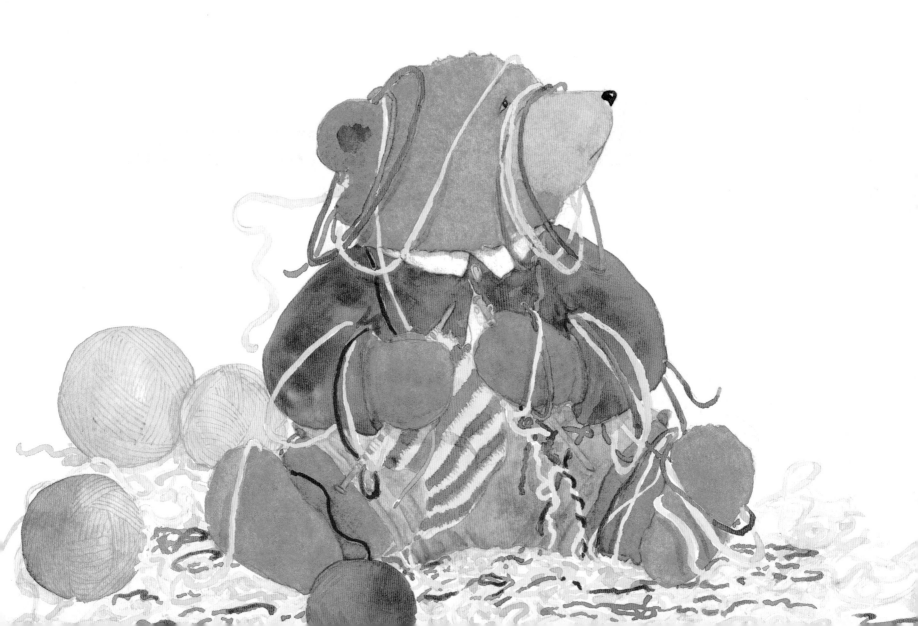

"Oh, dear. Maybe you could try the barbershop next door," suggested the sheep.

Little Brown Bear went to the barbershop. He took a deep breath and said, "I'm looking for a job."

The barber gave Little Brown Bear a comb and told him to get to work.

Little Brown Bear combed and snipped and buzzed. Then he handed the lion a mirror to admire his work.

"Roar!"

"What have you done?" asked the lion.
"Oops," said Little Brown Bear.

Little Brown Bear ran as fast as he could until he found himself right back at school. He wondered what his friends were doing, so he peeked in the window.

That looks like fun, he thought.

$$1 + 1 = 2$$
$$2 + 2 = 4$$

He tiptoed into the classroom and sat down at an empty table. The teacher came over to him and said, "I'm glad you're here. I have a job for you."

Oh, no, thought Little Brown Bear.

"We're going to learn how to write," said the teacher.
"Will you please hand out the paper?"
"I can do that!" said Little Brown Bear.

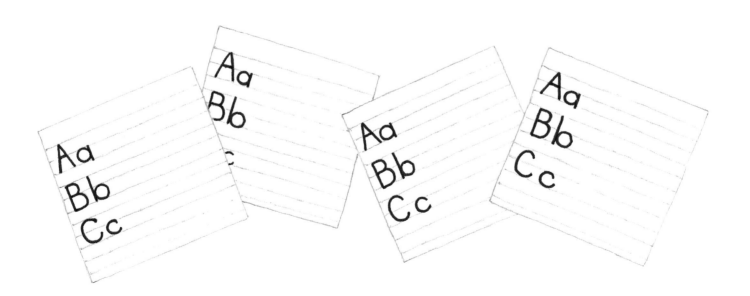